Summer

To Colin and Peedie P, of course

This edition published in 2011 by
Birlinn Limited
West Newington House
10 Newington Road
Edinburgh EH9 1QS

First published in 1989 by Bodley Head

www.birlinn.co.uk

Text and illustrations copyright
© Mairi Hedderwick 1989, 2011

ISBN: 978 1 78027 003 6

British Library Cataloguing-in-Publication Data
A catalogue record for this book is available
from the British Library

Page make-up by Mark Blackadder

Printed and bound in China

Peedie Peebles' Summer or Winter Book

Text and illustrations by Mairi Hedderwick

BIRLINN

Peedie Peebles likes waking everyone up early, SUMMER

or SUMMER. SUMMER or WINTER.

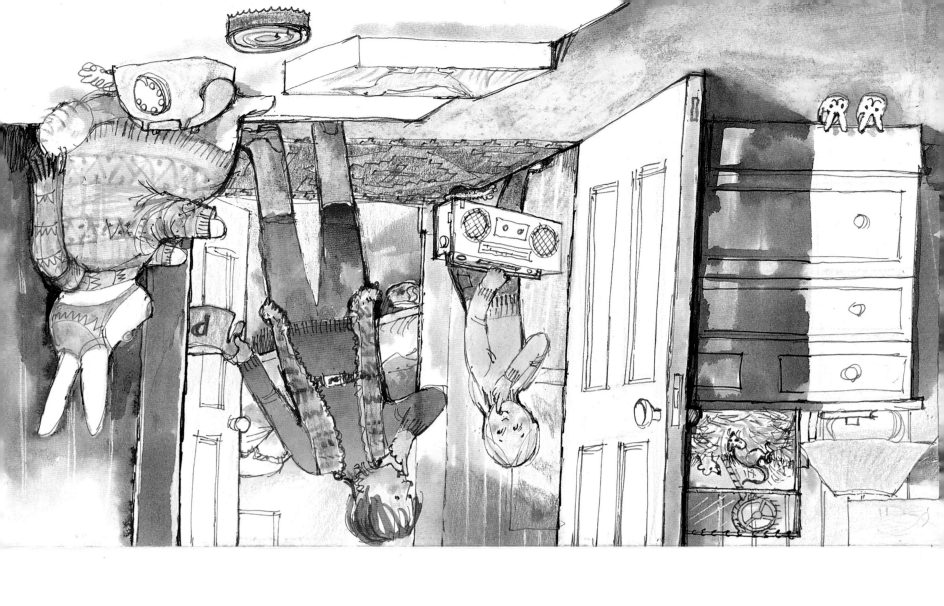

Winter

or WINTER.

And every time after that, Peedie Peebles falls fast asleep, WINTER

or SUMMER.

Until he remembers it is storytime, LOVELY time, SUMMER

or WINTER.

At bedtime Peedie Peebles is difficult to find, WINTER

or SUMMER.

Other times Peedie Peebles does WONDERFUL things, SUMMER

or WINTER.

Sometimes Peedie Peebles does DREADFUL things, WINTER

or SUMMER.

Breakfast is Peedie Peebles' favourite time, SUMMER

or WINTER.

Peedie Peebles does NOT like getting dressed, WINTER